TATTLIN' MADELINE

WRITTEN BY CAROL CUMMINGS · ILLUSTRATED BY JOSEPH NEWTON

The Get-Along Series

Other books and audiotapes available:

Copy the Cat
   ...learns please & thank you   (manners)

Finding Feelings (recognizing feelings)

I'm Always in Trouble (dealing with anger)

Won't You Ever Listen? (listening)

Sticks & Stones (giving compliments)

Sharing is Caring (sharing)

A Win-Win Day (problem solving)

About the Author

Dr. Carol Cummings conducts workshops for parents and teachers throughout the world on motivation, social skills, reading, effective teaching, classroom management, and cooperative learning. She has written over 16 books for teachers and children and teaches for Seattle Pacific University.

Published by: Teaching Inc.
               P.O. Box 788
               Edmonds, WA 98020
               (425) 774 0755

ISBN   0-9614574-4-9
           Printed in Taiwan

To parents and teachers

Take this opportunity to help children make friends. Research has shown that socially competent children are more accepted in school by their teachers and peers AND have higher achievement.

The goal of this book is to help children learn the difference between tattling and reporting. The suggestions that follow are to help you make the best use of this book.

Before you read

Ask questions to help children relate to things they already know about tattling.
•*We're going to read a story about a tattletale. What do you know about tattletales? Name everything that comes into your mind when you think of a tattletale.*
• *Have you ever called someone a tattletale? Why?*
• *Have you ever been called a tattletale? How did it make you feel?*
• *Look at the cover of this book. How do you think Madeline is feeling? Why?*
• *Do you think she likes being called "Tattlin' Madeline"?*
• *What do you think the book is going to be about? Let's see if you're right.*

While you read

Continue to ask questions.

p. 6   *What is Madeline's problem? Why is it a problem? How do you think she'll solve it? Let's see what happens.*

p. 12   *How did her teacher help her solve her problem? How is a tattletale different from a reporter? Do you think Madeline will be able to follow her teacher's advice? Let's see.*

p. 14   *If Madeline tells the teacher because she wants to get someone in trouble, what would she be called? If someone is playing with matches at school and Madeline tells the teacher, what would she be called? Why?*

p. 16   *Why didn't Madeline finish telling the teacher?*

p. 18   *What do you think Madeline did? Why? What could she say to her brother?*

p. 20   *Why was this the best day for Madeline?*

After you read

• *Provide more examples* of things that might happen to Madeline. Decide whether she'd tell the teacher or not. Always ask *WHY*! Ask if she could handle the problem herself. If so, what would she do/say?

    a. Someone bumps into her in line.

    b. A stranger is on the playground, asking lots of questions.

    c. Michael hits Madeline. (Be careful. Ask *when* it would be tattling and *when* it would be reporting.)

• *Ask questions related to the story structure* (or provide a writing activity)

    a. The problem in this story was....

    b. This was a problem because....

    c. The problem was finally solved when....

    d. In the end....

• *Activities*

    a. Write a story about tattling. You be the main character!

    b. Keep a journal about tattling. Provide sentence starters like:

        I don't want to be a tattletale because....

        Your friend called you "stupid." What could you do?

Tattlin' Madeline,
The kids all call me.
Tattlin' Madeline,
I don't want to be.

No one wants to be a tattletale, especially me! Tattletales don't have friends. In fact, when kids see me out at recess they say:

Madeline's no fun --
She tattles all the time.
So when she tattles,
We sing this rhyme.

Tattletale, tattletale,
Go away!
Tattletale, tattletale,
You can't play!

It happens all of the time. One day Nolen called me a name. So I told the teacher.

Teacher, teacher,
He said I'm dumb.
Teacher, teacher,
I saw him chewing gum.

Do you know what Nolen said then?

Tattlin' Madeline,
Go away!
Tattlin' Madeline,
You tattle all day!

It even happens at home. My little brother took my book. So I told my Mom.

Mommy, Mommy,
He took my book!
Mommy, Mommy,
Come and look!

Do you know what happened next? My little brother called me a tattletale.

Tattletale, tattletale,
Go away!
Tattletale, tattletale,
You can't play!

One day my teacher saw me sitting all alone at recess. I was crying. She wanted to know why.

"No one likes me. Not even my brother. Everyone calls me a tattletale."

My teacher told me a secret. She told me how to become a reporter and NOT a tattletale!

You want to become a reporter,
Not a tattletale, you say?
You want to have friends
Who invite you to play?

Reporters are the best.
They know what to do --
When to tell an adult
And when NOT to.

When you're really hurt or
Someone's in trouble,
GO REPORT
On the double!

When property will be damaged
And you can't stop it,
Reporters tell adults
All about it.

To get kids in trouble
Is why tattletales tell.
To get some attention
For themselves, as well.

So when you have a problem
You have to say,
Should this be reported
To an adult today?

Think about your problem --
Do you really need help?
Why must you tell the teacher --
Could you handle it yourself?

I wanted to put my reporter's cap on right away. My teacher said it wouldn't be easy. She said she'd give me a "T" signal to help me remember. I must think about **why I am TELLING her**.

Am I telling to get attention,
To get someone in trouble?
OR
Telling to get help
For someone on the double?

At our next recess, I asked some kids if I could play ball with them. They said no! Afterwards, when I ran up to my teacher to tattle, she gave me the signal. "Oops," I said. I didn't finish telling her. Do you know why?

At home, my brother was bugging me again. I wanted to tell my mom, but I remembered my secret. What do you think I did?

Today was one of the best. At recess, when the kids said I couldn't play, I just walked away and climbed on the bars. I didn't tell anyone!

Then, a few minutes later, one of the kids from the game asked ME if she could play.

Madeline, Madeline,
May I please play?
I'm tired of four square --
Let's climb today.

Does she know the secret
Between teacher and me,
That a tattletale is someone
I won't be?

If she is hurt or
Ever in trouble,
I'll be her friend --
Get help on the double.

Madeline's a good name after all.
If I report and don't tattle,
The kids won't call
me TATTLIN' MADELINE

...just Madeline.

Tattletale, tattletale,
Go away!
Tattletale, tattletale,
You can't play!

When you are hurt or
Someone's in trouble,
GO REPORT
On the double!

Tattletales like to tell on other kids to:

1. Get them into trouble.

2. Get attention for themselves.

Reporters report problems when:

1. Property will be damaged.

2. A person is going to be hurt.

(Permission is granted to enlarge the last two pages
for wall charts or student handouts.)